Farmer Joe's Hot Day

by **Nancy Wilcox Richards**

illustrated by
Werner Zimmermann

Scholastic Canada Ltd.
Toronto New York London Auckland Sydney
Mexico City New Delhi Hong Kong Buenos Aires

For Jamie, Hazel, Bob and Wil.
— N. W. R.

For Christopher, Tristan and Otto,
my pals and critics.
— W. Z.

Scholastic Canada Ltd.
604 King Street West, Toronto, Ontario M5V 1E1, Canada

Scholastic Inc.
557 Broadway, New York, NY 10012, USA

Scholastic Australia Pty Limited
PO Box 579, Gosford, NSW 2250, Australia

Scholastic New Zealand Limited
Private Bag 94407, Botany, Manukau 2163, New Zealand

Scholastic Children's Books
Euston House, 24 Eversholt Street, London NW1 1DB, UK

The illustrations were painted in watercolours on Arches paper.

Library and Archives Canada Cataloguing in Publication
Richards, Nancy Wilcox, 1958-
Farmer Joe's hot day / by Nancy Wilcox Richards ; illustrations by Werner Zimmermann.
ISBN 978-1-4431-1375-5
I. Zimmermann, H. Werner (Heinz Werner), 1951- II. Title.
PS8585.I184F3 2012   jC813'.54   C2011-908098-2

6 5 4 3 2 1   Printed in Singapore 46   12 13 14 15 16

Farmer Joe lived with his wife
in an old house
in the middle of a big field.

Every day Farmer Joe worked hard in the field.

He cut the wheat.
He planted the corn.
He pulled the weeds.
The sun shone down on him
and by the end of the day
he was hot and tired.

One day Farmer Joe
complained to his wife,
"Every day
I work hard in the field.

"I cut the wheat.
I plant the corn.
I pull the weeds.
The sun shines down on me
and by the end of the day
I am hot and tired.

What can I do?"

"Wear your jacket,"
said his wife.
"My jacket?" said Farmer Joe.
"Yes," said his wife.

So the next day

Farmer Joe put on his jacket
and off he went
to work in the field.

He cut the wheat.
He planted the corn.
The sun shone down on him
and before the end of the day
he was so hot and tired
that he could not
pull the weeds.

"What can I do?"
Farmer Joe complained
to his wife.

"Wear your coat," said his wife.
"My coat?" said Farmer Joe.
"Yes," said his wife.

So the next day

Farmer Joe put on his jacket
and his coat
and off he went
to work in the field.

He cut the wheat.
The sun shone down on him
and before the end of the day
he was so hot and tired
that he could not pull the weeds
or plant the corn.

"What can I do?"
Farmer Joe complained
to his wife.

"Wear your scarf and mittens,"
said his wife.

"My scarf and mittens?"
said Farmer Joe.

"Yes," said his wife.

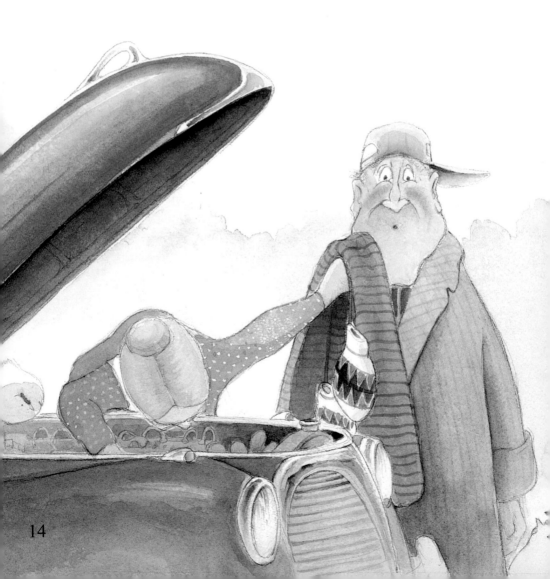

So the next day
Farmer Joe put on his jacket
and his coat
and his scarf and mittens
and off he went
to work in the field.

15

The sun shone down on him
and his jacket
and his coat
and his scarf and mittens.
He was so hot and tired
that he could not
cut the wheat
or plant the corn
or pull the weeds.

Farmer Joe was very angry.
"What can I do now?"
he asked his wife.

"I am so hot and tired
that I cannot work in the field."

"Take off your scarf
and mittens," said his wife.

"Take off your coat
and jacket."

"Take them off?"
said Farmer Joe.

"Yes," said his wife.

The next day
Farmer Joe worked hard
in the field.

He cut the wheat.
He planted the corn.
He pulled the weeds.

The sun shone down on him
and by the end of the day
he was hot and tired.

But . . .

he never complained
again!

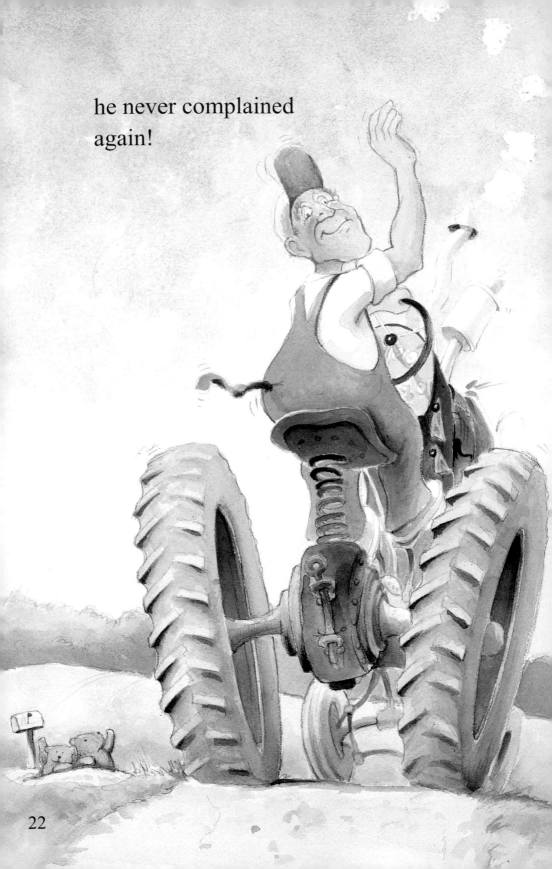